Dear Parents,

Welcome to the Scholastic Reader series. We have taken over 80 years of experience with teachers, parents, and children and put it into a program that is designed to match your child's interests and skills.

Level 1—Short sentences and stories made up of words kids can sound out using their phonics skills and words that are important to remember.

Level 2—Longer sentences and stories with words kids need to know and new "big" words that they will want to know.

Level 3—From sentences to paragraphs to longer stories, these books have large "chunks" of texts and are made up of a rich vocabulary.

Level 4—First chapter books with more words and fewer pictures.

It is important that children learn to read well enough to succeed in school and beyond. Here are ideas for reading this book with your child:

- Look at the book together. Encourage your child to read the title and make a prediction about the story.
- Read the book together. Encourage your child to sound out words when appropriate. When your child struggles, you can help by providing the word.
- Encourage your child to retell the story. This is a great way to check for comprehension.
- Have your child take the fluency test on the last page to check progress.

Scholastic Readers are designed to support your child's efforts to learn how to read at every age and every stage. Enjoy helping your child learn to read and love to read.

—**Francie Alexander**
    Chief Education Officer
    Scholastic Education

Text copyright © 2004 by Scholastic Inc.
Illustrations copyright © 2004 by Barbara Lanza.
All rights reserved. Published by Scholastic Inc.
SCHOLASTIC, CARTWHEEL BOOKS, and associated logos are trademarks and/or registered trademarks of Scholastic Inc.

Library of Congress Cataloging-in-Publication Data
Lewis, Hara.
  Cinderella / Hara Lewis, author ; Barbara Lanza, illustrator.
    p. cm. — (Scholastic readers. Level 2)
  Summary: In her haste to flee the palace before the fairy godmother's magic loses effect, Cinderella leaves behind a glass slipper, providing a clue for the prince who has fallen in love with her.
  ISBN 0-439-47153-2 (pbk. : alk. paper)
  [1. Fairy tales. 2. Folklore.] I. Lanza, Barbara, ill. II. Title. III. Series.
PZ8.L48114Ci 2004
398.2'0944'02 — dc21   2003004561

10 9 8 7 6 5 4 3 2 1   04 05 06 07 08
         Printed in the U.S.A. 23 • First printing, February 2004

Cinderella

by **Hara Lewis**

Illustrated by **Barbara Lanza**

Scholastic Reader — Level 2

SCHOLASTIC INC.

New York   Toronto   London   Auckland   Sydney
Mexico City   New Delhi   Hong Kong   Buenos Aires

There once was a beautiful girl named Cinderella.

Cinderella had a mean stepmother and two ugly stepsisters. They made her cook and clean and wear ragged clothes.

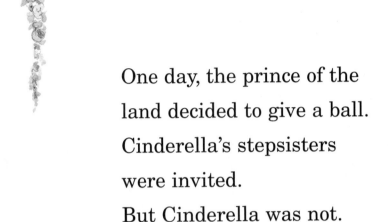

One day, the prince of the
land decided to give a ball.
Cinderella's stepsisters
were invited.
But Cinderella was not.

The sisters tried on dresses to wear.
They made Cinderella fix their hair.

"Cinderella, wouldn't you love to go
to the ball?" they asked, laughing.
"I wish I could go,"
Cinderella cried softly.

Soon it was the night of the ball.
The stepsisters rushed off to the palace.
Cinderella sat alone, crying.

Just then, her fairy godmother appeared.

"I will help you go to the ball, Cinderella."

The fairy godmother tapped
seven mice with her wand.
They turned into six fine horses
and a jolly coachman.

Then she waved her wand
over a pumpkin.
It turned into a fancy coach.

She waved her wand
once more.
Cinderella's torn dress
turned into a beautiful gown.
And pretty glass slippers
appeared on her feet.

"Now you must hurry,"
said the fairy godmother.
"The spell will end
at midnight.
You must return home
before the clock
strikes twelve!"

At the ball, the prince danced
only with Cinderella.
No one knew that Cinderella
was the beautiful princess.

The clock struck twelve.

It was midnight.

The spell was about to end!

Cinderella forgot about the time.

Cinderella ran from the palace.
One of her glass slippers fell
on the steps.

The prince ran after Cinderella.

He could not catch her.

He picked up the slipper

and went back to the ball.

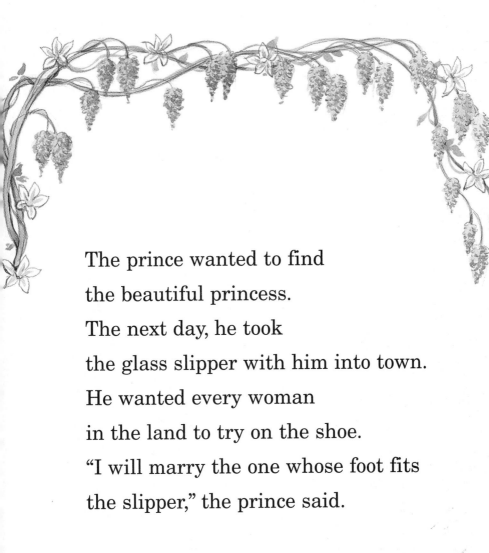

The prince wanted to find
the beautiful princess.
The next day, he took
the glass slipper with him into town.
He wanted every woman
in the land to try on the shoe.
"I will marry the one whose foot fits
the slipper," the prince said.

The prince reached Cinderella's house.
Her mean stepsisters pushed Cinderella aside.

They each tried on the slipper.

It did not fit.

"May I try?"
Cinderella asked.
Her stepsisters
laughed at her.
But the prince
placed the shoe
on her foot.
It fit perfectly!

Cinderella pulled the other slipper
from her pocket.
She slid it on.
Her sisters were shocked.

Suddenly, her fairy godmother appeared.
She turned Cinderella's ragged dress
into a lovely gown.

"You are the one I danced with!"
said the prince to Cinderella.
"Will you marry me?" he asked.
"Yes," said Cinderella.

And Cinderella and the prince
lived happily ever after.

Fluency Fun

The words in each list below end in the same sounds.
Read the words in a list.
Read them again.
Read them faster.
Try to read all 15 words in one minute.

block	**gown**	**bright**
clock	**brown**	**flight**
flock	**crown**	**might**
knock	**drown**	**nightly**
pocket	**frown**	**midnight**

Look for these words in the story.

once **beautiful** **woman**

alone **whose**

Note to Parents:

According to *A Dictionary of Reading and Related Terms*, fluency is "the ability to read smoothly, easily, and readily with freedom from word-recognition problems." Fluency is necessary for good comprehension and enjoyable reading. The activities on this page include a speed drill and a sight-recognition drill. Speed drills build fluency because they help students rapidly recognize common syllables and spelling patterns in words, and they're fun! Sight-recognition drills help students smoothly and accurately recognize words. Practice these activities with your child to help him or her become a fluent reader.

—**Wiley Blevins,**
Reading Specialist